This book belongs to

_____

Skagway

Juneau

Petersburg

Sitka

Wrangell

Ketchikan

JOHN MUIR and STICKEEN

An Icy Adventure with a No-Good Dog

by JULIE DUNLAP AND MARYBETH LORBIECKI
illustrated by BILL FARNSWORTH

NORTHWORD PRESS
CHANHASSEN, MINNESOTA

Though this story is based
on the writings and journals of John Muir,
the journals in the illustrations
are not meant to be reproductions
of Muir's journals.

The native men in Muir's crew were
Stickeen, or Stikine, Indians—
members of a larger native group called
the Tlingit people.

To Nathan and Eli,
wishing you many wild adventures together
—J.D.

For Dad, for raising us as campers
for Mom, for making the trips possible
for Cooper, our Stickeen
—M.L.

For my wife, Debbie, and my daughters,
Allison and Caitlin
—B.F.

The illustrations were rendered in oils on linen
The text type was set in Elegant Garamond
The display type was set in Birch, Tiger Rag and Zapfino
Composed in the United States of America
Designed by Lois A. Rainwater
Edited by Aimee Jackson

Totem pole illustration based on a drawing from John Muir Papers,
Holt-Atherton Special Collections, University of the Pacific Libraries.
© 1984 Muir-Hanna Trust.

Text © 2004 by Julie Dunlap and Marybeth Lorbiecki
Illustrations © 2004 by Bill Farnsworth

Books for Young Readers
NorthWord Press
18705 Lake Drive East
Chanhassen, MN 55317
www.northwordpress.com

Library of Congress Cataloging-in-Publication Data: Pending

Printed in Singapore
10 9 8 7 6 5 4 3 2 1

Come along on a trip to Alaska...

IT'S 1880 AND FEW AMERICAN citizens have ventured up into Alaska, unless they are after gold. But John Muir isn't after gold, he's after ice! He is out to map glaciers—age-old rivers of slowly moving ice.

He loves anything wild.

And he wants nothing to do with pets—especially the no-good, stubborn, troublemaking dog, Stickeen, that his friend wants to bring along. This is the true story of Muir's voyage, based on his writings and journals.

John Muir was born in Scotland in 1838. He spoke with an accent and used many Scottish expressions, like "ye" instead of "you."

At the time of this Alaska trip, John Muir was not famous. He hadn't yet convinced President Roosevelt to create a national park in California, or helped to start the Sierra Club—a group dedicated to wilderness adventures and protecting wild places. But he had been a farmer, inventor, and wanderer through swamps, across prairies, and over mountains. And people did know his name as a newspaper writer. His reports of daring climbs, bone-rattling storms, and canoe trips in search of lost glaciers thrilled readers across the country.

Muir had even herded sheep so he could live day and night in the mountains. He carefully watched the deer, eagles, coyotes, and grizzlies there. He learned to hate the sheep and cattle for gobbling and trampling the mountain meadows. John was sure tame animals had lost the quick brains and bold spirits he admired in wild ones.

That is, until one determined dog changed his mind.

John Muir stared at his friend's dog. Silky hair. Dainty paws. And darkness in his eyes, like weather that could turn on you.

"Yer pet doesn't belong on this trip," John complained. "He'll need care like a baby."

Hall Young just laughed. "Stickeen's a wonder of a dog, Muir. He can swim like a seal, stand cold like a bear."

John scoffed. But the dog jumped into the boat. That's how much Stickeen cared for John Muir's opinion.

"Ut-ha! Pull!" The expedition was off—to map Alaska's glaciers.

The men leaned into their oars. John jotted notes and sketched. He drew gulls slicing through the breeze and porpoises arching above the waves. This was the life!

Then a thunderous crack echoed—CRRRRRRRRCH! A chunk of glacier slammed into the water. Icy waves shot up. The canoe rocked.

Everyone fought to keep the canoe from tipping. Everyone except Stickeen, his snout on the prow.

The waters finally quieted.

John glanced at the sopping-wet dog. *Just as I thought. A lazy, coddled pet, waiting for a towel-rub.*

Stickeen saw John's eyes on him. He crawled under Muir's legs, then shook himself dry.

Hall and the crew hooted while John dripped.

August 8, 1880,

Expedition:
  Fort Wrangell to Glacier Bay,
  Alaska Territory
Purpose: to map uncharted glaciers
Expedition leaders:
  John Muir, writer and explorer
  S. Hall Young,
    Presbyterian missionary
  Lot Tyeen,
    Tlinget crew captain
Extra baggage:
  One worthless dog, Stickeen

Wildlife sighting:
  Feathered people

At every landing, Stickeen was the first out. The dog went where he wanted and ignored all calls to leave. At the last moment, there would be Stickeen, paddling to catch up.

He's not my problem, thought John.

His mind was on the wild mountains of ice. Muir had such a crazy love of glaciers, the natives called him *Glate Ankow,* "Ice Chief."

At each camp, John tramped into the forest and over mountains, scribbling notes along the way. And who began tagging along?

Stickeen!

"Get on with ye," John shouted. "Ye're not fit for the wild!" He waved his arms. He threw pinecones. He ignored the dog.

Nothing worked.

Every day, there he'd be, that dog, following Muir. Not close enough to be friendly. Never a tail wag. Never a lick or a look or a bark of greetings.

Stickeen seemed as cold and silent as a glacier.

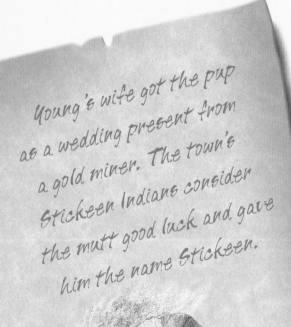

Young's wife got the pup as a wedding present from a gold miner. The town's Stickeen Indians consider the mutt good luck and gave him the name Stickeen.

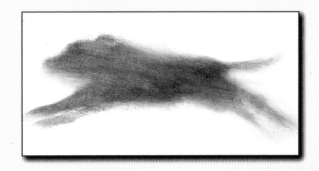

One night, John and Lot left camp in the dark to catch supper. Thousands of salmon fins churned the stream into silver fire. Then from a far bank came a steady comet-like blaze toward them—like a huge beast chasing the fishermen. Lot rowed hard.

Inches from the boat, the "monster" lifted its head. Muir roared with laughter. "Stickeen!"

What a puzzle was that bothering little dog.

❄ ❄ ❄

The last morning in Glacier Bay was as wild and dark as an angry grizzly. Tomorrow, the expedition would have to turn for home. The ice called to Muir, rousing him from a deep sleep. He slipped from the tent, careful not to wake the others or Stickeen.

I meant to gulp some coffee before starting out, but when I heard the storm and looked out I made haste to join it, for many of Nature's finest lessons are to be found in her storms.

Not far from camp, John spotted a shadow slipping behind him through the trees.

"Go back to camp and have yer breakfast!" John yelled. "This storm will kill ye!"

But Muir should have known. Stickeen was more stubborn than he. Beaten, John offered the drenched dog a bit of his biscuit.

John hiked up rocky slopes, leaving the dog to do as he wished. A shaft of sun split the storm. Ahead stood the king of glaciers!

Strange that Stickeen would have ventured forth this stormy day when all the other wolves were glad to stay home in the rocks and woods.

Bloody tracks on the ice told me the glacier had torn the doggie's paws, so I fashioned him some moccasins from handkerchiefs. Just tied them on, and he was off again as usual.

Hacking ice-steps with his ax, Muir climbed the blue wall. Stickeen scrambled after. On top, an endless sheet of ice stretched before them.

John hiked and sketched for hours, with an eye on the sky. He skipped over small ice cracks and zigzagged around deep crevasses. Stickeen followed.

The clouds blackened again. Muir had to hurry back to camp or face a night on the glacier without tent or fire. He ran hard through the swarming snow, the dog close at his heels. Both were hungry, soaked, and aching from cold.

Then John stopped. Stickeen looked up at him. It was as if the dog knew.

Muir was lost.

Backtracking, John used lines in the ice and wind direction to find his way. Stickeen tracked him like a trooper. At one broad gash, Muir peered down, down, down. Only one spot was narrow enough to leap across. And the far side was much lower. If he jumped down, he could never jump back up.

John hurdled across and down, wobbling on the slippery edge. Stickeen landed after Muir, not a hair to spare. But he trotted on, unrattled. Did nothing scare this dog?

Within minutes, the widest crack yet blocked their way. They were marooned on an island of ice.

Kneeling, John saw one slim chance of escape. Far below, a sagging sliver of ice bridged the chasm. Could it hold their weight?

Stickeen nudged his shoulder. "Hush yer fears, wee beastie," John crooned softly.

Chip, chip, chip. He carved one heel hold, then another, down the ice-canyon's wall.

Ever so slowly, Muir lowered his body onto the sagging bridge.

It held.

Stickeen paced the rim. He began to whimper.

Legs dangling, John shaved flat the ice before him. He hitched himself forward, smoothing a path two-paws wide.

Mournful cries called to him from above.

Somehow, John's cold-clumsy hands cut a ladder up the other side of the canyon and he hauled himself out of danger. But he didn't rejoice.

He looked back for the dog. Could that pitiful creature, wailing and pacing, be Stickeen? "Come on, come on," Muir pleaded. "Ye can do it, wee boy!"

Then Stickeen lay down. His howls dipped and screeched.

John tried ordering him. "Stop yer nonsense!"

Shaking, Stickeen replied with more miserable wails.

Time was running out. With nightfall, Stickeen would likely fall or freeze to death. Could John return to camp for help and grope his way back in the dark?

No. The dog had to do it on his own. Now.

"Stickeen, poor boy," Muir said. "Don't ye see there's nothing I can do!"

The dog did not stir.

It was the last thing in the world he wanted to do, but John turned and walked away.

Stickeen's howls pierced the wind as Muir's back disappeared in the swirling gloom.

Stickeen's cries and shivers drained away. He pressed himself against the ice and slid his front paws, then his back, over the edge. Hair by hair, down each step.

Then a final sliding of muscle and fur, and he made it to the little bridge of ice.

But how far he still had to go! His tail fell to half mast. His body began to shake, more fiercely than before. The wind sharpened, nearly pushing Stickeen off the ice bridge.

Then the dog glanced up at the rim.

Had the danger been less, his distress would have seemed ridiculous. But in this dismal, merciless abyss lay the shadow of death. We were forced to face it.

No right way is easy in this rough world. We must risk our lives to save them.

John was peering down. He had never really left.

The dog's tail flew over his back. Steady as the pelting snow, Stickeen moved over John's bridge-way path.

But at the wall, Stickeen stopped and eyed the towering cliff. Dogs are poor climbers, John knew.

Would Stickeen try?

Stickeen launched skyward, scrabbling up the wall and over the top.

"Well done," John cheered. "Well done, my boy!" He reached out for the dog, but Stickeen whizzed past, whirling, dancing, rolling head over heels. Squealing, the dog spun and charged at John, nearly knocking him down. A gleam in Stickeen's eyes shouted, "Saved! Saved at last!"

Nothing could frighten them now. All the cracks they met seemed puny and easily hopped.

Through the darkness, they spotted Lot's campfire.
Stickeen staggered to a blanket by the fire.
The men rubbed John dry as he spun out the tale of their storm battle for life. Stickeen had proven that his spirit was as fine as any wild creature's—or any human's.
"Yon's a brave doggie," John declared, nodding to Stickeen. Stickeen answered with a heavy thump of his tail.

Stickeen was a changed dog, always ready to rest his head on my knee. And often as he caught my eye he seemed to be trying to say, "Wasn't that an awful time we had together on the glacier?"

Expedition completed: September, 1880
Wildlife seen: porpoises, gulls, salmon, ravens, foxes, ducks, wolves, mountain goats, grizzlies.
Finest animal of all: Stickeen the dog...enlarged the boundaries of my life. I saw through him down into the depths of our common nature.

Afterword...

For the rest of their voyage, the dog sat by John in the canoe by day and slept by his side at night. Stickeen and the Ice Chief endured many more adventures on the trip south.

At Sitka, Alaska, John had to leave his companions to catch a steamship home to California. The crew had to hold the struggling dog while John stepped onto the pier. Stickeen stood in the canoe—howling, howling—his mournful good-bye carried on the winds.

John never forgot his brave friend. Muir devoted himself to protecting wild lands, talking to presidents, giving speeches, and writing books about our need for nature's freedom and beauty. But he always had time to tell his favorite tale of Stickeen's struggle for life on the ice in Glacier Bay. He called their adventure "the most memorable of all my wild days."

In two books written late in life, *Stickeen* and *My Boyhood and Youth*, Muir urged readers to love all of the Earth's creatures, both wild and tame. Stickeen had shown something to Muir. Animals were much more like humans than John had thought. In Stickeen, the Ice Chief had found his kindred spirit.

Barrow

Prudhoe Bay

Arctic Circle

Nome

Alaska

Fairbanks

Tok

Bethel

Glennallen

Dillingham

Anchorage

King Salmon

Homer

Valdez

Kodiak